Bedtime,

Nelly!

Jan Barger

ꕹ Charlesbridge

for Sam
—J. B.

Published by Charlesbridge
85 Main Street
Watertown, MA 02472
(617) 926-0329
www.charlesbridge.com

Library of Congress Cataloging-in-Publication Data
Barger, Jan, 1948-
   Bedtime, Nelly! / Jan Barger.
      p. cm.
   Summary: It is Nelly's bedtime, but first she has to
say her goodnights.
   ISBN 1-58089-094-6 (reinforced for library use)
   [1. Bedtime—Fiction.] I. Title.
   PZ7.B250373Be 2004
   [E]—dc22

                              2003015843

Printed in China
(hc) 10 9 8 7 6 5 4 3 2 1

Illustrations done in watercolor and pencil on paper
Display type and text type set in Argenta
Color separations by Ocean Graphic Company Ltd.
Printed and bound by Everbest Printing Co. Ltd through
   Four Colour Imports Ltd., Louisville, Kentucky
Production supervision by Brian G. Walker
Designed by Diane M. Earley

"Bedtime, Nelly," said Mommy.

"First I have to say goodnight to the stars," said Nelly.

"Goodnight, stars," said Nelly.

"Do they say goodnight to you?" asked Mommy.

"They do if they can," said Nelly. "Sometimes they're behind a cloud, and they can't."

"Bedtime, Nelly," said Daddy.

"First I have to say goodnight to my pets," said Nelly.

"Goodnight, Dog,"
said Nelly.

"Goodnight, Cat.

Goodnight, Parrot.

Goodnight, Guinea Pig.

Goodnight, Fish."

"Do they say goodnight
to you?" asked Daddy.

"Bedtime, Nelly," said Granny.

"First I have to say goodnight to my toys," said Nelly.

"Goodnight, Woolly," said Nelly.
"Goodnight, Moocow.

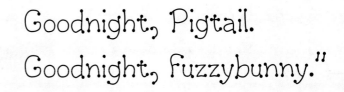

Goodnight, Pigtail.
Goodnight, Fuzzybunny."

"Do they say goodnight to you?" asked Granny.

"Toys don't say goodnight,"
said Nelly. "Not unless you
say it for them."

"Bedtime, Nelly," said Mommy,
"and no more goodnights!"

"But," said Nelly, "I still have
to say goodnight to . . .

". . . you! Goodnight."